D0574187

CALGARY PUBLIC LIBRARY

JUL

LOST
and
FOUND

by
Rebecca Doughty

G. P. PUTNAM'S SONS • NEW YORK

G. P. PUTNAM'S SONS
A division of Penguin Young Readers Group
Published by The Penguin Group
Penguin Group (USA) Inc., 375 Hudson Street, New York, NY 10014, U.S.A.
Penguin Group (Canada), 10 Alcorn Avenue, Toronto, Ontario, Canada M4V 3B2 (a division of Pearson Penguin Canada Inc.)
Penguin Books Ltd, 80 Strand, London WC2R 0RL, England.
Penguin Ireland, 25 St. Stephen's Green, Dublin 2, Ireland (a division of Penguin Books Ltd.)
Penguin Books India Pvt Ltd, 11 Community Centre, Panchsheel Park, New Delhi - 110 017, India.
Penguin Group (NZ), Cnr Airborne and Rosedale Roads, Albany, Auckland, New Zealand (a division of Pearson New Zealand Ltd).
Penguin Books (South Africa) (Pty) Ltd, 24 Sturdee Avenue, Rosebank, Johannesburg 2196, South Africa.
Penguin Books Ltd, Registered Offices: 80 Strand, London WC2R 0RL, England.

Copyright © 2005 by Rebecca Doughty.
All rights reserved. This book, or parts thereof, may not be reproduced in any form without permission in writing from the publisher,
G. P. Putnam's Sons, a division of Penguin Young Readers Group, 345 Hudson Street, New York, NY 10014.
G. P. Putnam's Sons, Reg. U.S. Pat. & Tm. Off. The scanning, uploading and distribution of this book via the Internet or
via any other means without the permission of the publisher is illegal and punishable by law.
Please purchase only authorized electronic editions, and do not participate in or encourage electronic piracy of copyrighted materials.
Your support of the author's rights is appreciated.

Published simultaneously in Canada. Manufactured in China by South China Printing Co. Ltd.
Designed by Marikka Tamura. Text set in Melvin Sans Regular.
The art was done in Flashe paint and ink on bristol board.
Library of Congress Cataloging-in-Publication Data
Doughty, Rebecca, 1955-
Lost and found / Rebecca Doughty. p. cm.
Summary: When Lucy slows down, she finds that she does not lose things as much as she used to.
[1. Lost and found possessions—Fiction. 2. Speed—Fiction. 3. Stories in rhyme.] I. Title.
PZ8.3.D743Lo 2005   [E]–dc22
2004018203
ISBN 0-399-24177-9
1 3 5 7 9 10 8 6 4 2
First Impression

for Deb

beep
beep

I was late again,
couldn't find my shoes.

so I had to wear the ones
I didn't lose.

On the bus I lost my book.

My sister Lizzy
helped me look.

Getting off the bus, I lost my snack.

it must have fallen
out of my pack.

I lost my homework.

no really it's true!

It must have fallen out of there too.

Well, then my teacher said:

"Lucy, if you weren't always in a rush,

you might not lose things quite as much."

But I *had* to rush to keep up in the race!
Then I tripped and fell and got mud on my face.

I lost my jacket and Mom said:

"You'd lose your HEAD if it wasn't on tight!"

And I got grumpy.
I knew she was right.

I lost my temper
and started to shout.

time-out.

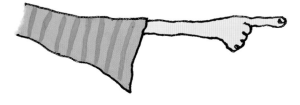

then I lost some playtime
and couldn't go out!

When I got tired of being a crankyhead,

I went exploring
under my bed.

And what do you think I found down there?

A shoe,
a sock,
some underwear,

my favorite book,
a baseball bat,

my bunny slipper,
my cowboy hat,

pens and pencils,
and this and that.

Ted ♥

bunny too!

stuff

stuff

Scout's bone

more stuff

Stuff I'd lost was all around.
I found a lot when I slowed down.

But wait a minute!

Where did my dog go?
Where did he hide?

I left the door open and he ran outside!

I was so upset,
I started to cry.

But then I knew
I had to try . . .

so I got to work
and put up a sign.

are
you
Lucy?

and somebody found
that dog of mine!

Now I had Scout back and someone new.
I found a good friend on that day too.

The next day at school

I looked all around.

and there was my jacket in the lost-and-found.

You know, I think I'd rather choose

hmmm...

to take the time to find, not lose!